P9-AQD-524

DATE DUE

Demco, Inc. 38-293

Library and Archives Canada Cataloguing in Publication

Ryan, Tom, 1977-
Totally unrelated / Tom Ryan.
(Orca limelights)

Issued also in electronic format.
ISBN 978-1-4598-0458-6 (pbk.). – ISBN 9781459806481 (bound).

I. Title. II. Series: Orca limelights
PS8635.Y359T67 2013   jc813'.6   C2013-901913-8

First published in the United States, 2013
Library of Congress Control Number: 2013935383

Summary: When Neil starts to compose and play his own music, it conflicts
with the traditional Celtic music he performs with his family's band.

*Orca Book Publishers is dedicated to preserving the environment and has
printed this book on Forest Stewardship Council® certified paper.*

Orca Book Publishers gratefully acknowledges the support for
its publishing programs provided by the following agencies:
the Government of Canada through the Canada Book Fund and the
Canada Council for the Arts, and the Province of British Columbia
through the BC Arts Council and the Book Publishing Tax Credit.

Design by Teresa Bubela
Cover photography by Getty Images

ORCA BOOK PUBLISHERS
PO Box 5626, STN. B
Victoria, BC Canada
V8R 6S4

ORCA BOOK PUBLISHERS
PO Box 468
Custer, WA USA
98240-0468

www.orcabook.com
Printed and bound in Canada.

16 15 14 13 • 4 3 2 1

For Liam, Calum and James, the best brothers
I ever could have asked for.

One

I t'd be a lot easier to kill Bert, my best buddy since kindergarten, if I could find the guy. I know he's somewhere in this massive abandoned warehouse—there's no way out, for either of us. I'm locked and loaded and adrenaline is coursing through my veins, but if he tracks me down first, none of that matters.

I move slowly down the dimly lit hallway, my back against the wall. When I get to the corner where the corridor makes a right turn, I stop and take a second to gather my nerves, then quickly flip around and make my move, hoping to catch him by surprise. Unfortunately, Bert has the same idea, and before I realize what's happening, he's jumped out in front of me from behind a pile of packing crates.

I yell as I start shooting, but he's too quick for me, and the bazooka he's packing unloads, tossing me backward in slow motion. I slam into a pile of rubble as *Game Over Sucker* scrolls across the screen to the sound of some kind of futuristic sad trombone. I whip my joystick at the couch on the other side of the room and try to ignore Bert's hoots and hollers. Not always the easiest task, considering he's the loudest person I know.

"Yes!" he yells. "Yes! Yes! Eat my dust, loser!"

I get up to leave.

"Aw, c'mon," he says. "One more game."

"Sorry, man," I say, grabbing my hoodie from the couch. "Gotta bounce. Big family dinner tonight."

Bert's an only child, and, as annoying as he can be, his basement is pretty much my refuge from the world, especially during the summer. He even has his own bathroom. It usually stinks, but still. My house is packed to the rafters—one senior citizen; two middle-agers; three, sometimes four, teenagers; and two preteen girls in a four-bedroom house with one and a half bathrooms. You do the math.

"You guys have a big family dinner every night," he says.

"Yeah, but Kathy gets home from college today, so my parents want everyone there."

"Oh, really?" he says. "How's old Kathy doing, anyway?" I know this isn't an innocent question. Bert has been in love with my older sister since the moment girls stopped being gross.

"I haven't seen her yet," I tell him. "She's supposed to land this afternoon sometime."

"Make sure she knows I'm around in case she's feeling lonely."

"Whatever, man," I say. "Catch you later."

I'm already halfway up the stairs when he yells after me, "Oh hey, Neil, wait!"

"What?" I call back over my shoulder.

"Seriously, come here for a minute. I want to show you something!"

Reluctantly, I walk back down and stand in the doorway. "What is it? I'm going to be late."

He rummages in a pile of crap on the coffee table and pulls out a page torn from the newspaper. "I almost forgot," he says. He leaps over the back of the couch and shoves the paper at me. "Check this out."

He's circled an item in the community-announcements section with red pen. *Deep Cove Talent Show*, the caption reads.

"Talent show?" I ask. "What, are you going to start juggling or something?"

"No, man," he says. "Keep reading."

"'To help commemorate the twenty-fifth anniversary of Deep Cove Days, there will be a live talent show on the waterfront,'" I read aloud. "'Three judges will choose the winner from local acts. Deadline for registration is July fifth. Grand prize five hundred dollars.'"

"What do you think, man?" he asks. "Seriously."

"I don't know," I say. "What are you planning on doing?"

"You mean, what are *we* planning on doing?"

"Yeah right," I say, handing him back the paper. "You want to do a magic routine? Saw me up in a wooden box?"

"No, man," he says, frustrated. "We'll start a band, like we've always talked about."

"I don't think we've ever talked about starting a band, Bert."

"Sure we have! Remember when we had to watch that stupid documentary about Bieber at

Joanie's birthday party and you were all like, '*We could do a better job than that guy*'?"

"I'm pretty sure I was joking," I say.

"Okay, whatever, but you can really play, Neil! All you need to do is learn a couple of songs that people actually want to listen to, for a change. Come on. I know you're dying to finally play some real music. Use your powers for good, Neil. Think about it."

I make a face at him. I won't lie; I've always wanted to play music I actually like, but banging out tunes with Bert for a talent show isn't really what I had in mind. "What are you going to play?" I ask.

"Drums, meathead!" He points to a huge pile of clothes in the corner of the basement, and I'm reminded that, yes, there is a drum set under there.

"Bert," I say, "you've played those twice in your life. If that."

"Well, there's no time like the present," he says. "Besides, I've been practicing. Wanna hear?"

"I'm good," I tell him.

"Look," he says, "the show is in a month. You know we can get one good song down by then. I'll drum and do the lead vocals too."

"Yeah right," I say. "I've heard you sing. Forget about it."

"Okay, fine, so we find ourselves a singer, give ourselves a name and there you go, we're rock stars."

I look at the announcement again. The show is on a Thursday, which is my only guaranteed day off from work. Against my better judgment, I begin to soften.

"Let me think about it," I say. "I really have to go."

"What's the big rush? It's only three o'clock—you won't be eating for a few hours."

"Dad wants us to squeeze in a practice before dinner," I tell him, knowing exactly how Bert will react.

Sure enough, he grins and breaks into a spastic dance, kind of a cross between an Irish jig and a Russian wedding dance.

"Fiddle dee deedle dee deedle dee doo," he yells gleefully, spinning in a circle and kicking wildly, his bent arms flapping in and out.

"Yep, that's what we do at practice, Bert," I say, doing my best to ignore him. It's no use. He's graduated to flying kicks.

I turn to head back up the stairs, pretending not to hear him as he yells after me, "Don't forget to come visit when you're done playing the bagpipes!" The last thing I hear as the screen door to his porch slams behind me is what sounds like a goose singing "The Star-Spangled Banner" during mating season. Good old Bert.

Two

I bomb up the driveway on my bike. I can already hear the squeak and whistle of the sound system being tweaked in the garage.

I lean my bike against the side of the building and come around front. The garage door is open, and I can see right away that, as usual, I'm the last to arrive. Everyone else is already in there, moving around, all business, running like a well-oiled machine. I stand at the corner of the door, watching them for a moment before they notice me. Dad is going over some sheet music with my mom and my older brother, Shamus, who's seventeen and ready to enter his senior year of high school. Molly and Maura, the twins, are in the corner of the room, practicing some dance steps for Kathy. She stands back and scrutinizes them, suggesting small changes. The twins look pretty scrawny and goofy in black leggings, their masses of red curls pulled back into scrunchies, but their faces are serious as they listen to what Kathy tells them. On the opposite side of the room, my younger brother, Johnny, lies practically upside down in a beat-up old armchair, cleaning the mouthpiece on his chanter.

The Family McClintock, they call us. That might sound kind of obvious, since (a) we're a family and (b) our last name is McClintock, but we're not just any old family McClintock. We're *the* family McClintock. Our name doesn't just show up on our phone bill; it gets printed in the papers and on the websites that promote our shows. It gets spelled out in big block letters on announcement boards outside the schools and community centers where we play most of our gigs, and it pops boldly off the covers of our self-produced CDs, which fill cardboard boxes in our garage.

We play traditional Celtic music—have for about ten years, since I was five. At first we just played small local shows around our hometown, Deep Cove, Nova Scotia, but a few years ago things took off and we found ourselves getting requests to do performances up and down the coast of Cape Breton Island. Now we're booked solid for most of the summer season, sometimes even driving off the island to do concerts and festivals in other parts of the Maritimes. We always get a good reception; tourists love good old-fashioned fiddling and stepdancing.

Not that that's all we do. Kathy has a voice like an angel and uses it to belt out the sweetest Gaelic tunes you ever heard. Shamus can really kick it on the bodhran, a traditional Celtic drum. Johnny pulls beautiful sounds out of the bagpipes, and no, I'm not being sarcastic. Trust me—it's even harder than it sounds. The twins are famous not only for their stepdancing but also for their Highland fling, which they execute like a pair of Olympic-level synchronized swimmers in kilts.

And, of course, there are my parents. My mom's confident, rollicking piano playing and my dad's energetic fiddling are the backbone of the whole operation. If you go back far enough, this is really how things got started. Dad likes to tell the story of how he and Mom met. He was playing at a square dance, and his piano player got the stomach flu and had to bail. My dad yelled into the crowd to see if anyone could carry a tune, and our mom, who'd learned piano sitting on her grandfather's knee, just happened to be there. She stepped up to the plate, and apparently they liked more than each other's playing. Eventually they got married and started popping out musical babies, and the rest is history.

Yep, the Family McClintock is an impressive bunch, that's for sure, and perhaps the most amazing thing about my parents and siblings is that every single one of them is multitalented. They all play at least three instruments. Give Molly a penny whistle and toss a mandolin to Shamus, and they'll both figure out what to do with them. Drag a harp in front of Kathy, and she'll strum like there's no tomorrow. I'm pretty sure that if someone were to throw a didgeridoo onstage at one of our shows, it'd be incorporated into the mix by the end of the set—"Waltzing MacTilda" or something like that.

Kathy is the first to see me, and she rushes over to give me a hug.

"It's so good to see you," she says.

"You too," I tell her. Kathy and I get along really well. "What gives, anyway?" I ask her.

"I thought your exams ended weeks ago. How come it took you so long to get home?"

"Long story," she whispers. "I'll fill you in later."

"Late again, Neil," says Dad. "Not a good start to the season." He's a stickler for showing up on time, so I often end up disappointing him. I'm glad that he doesn't make a big deal out of it today. Everybody is happy that Kathy is finally home.

My dad claps his hands. "Okay, everyone, grab your gear. Get into place."

I'm sure by this point you're asking what exactly it is that *I* do. Well, for one thing, I don't dance, that's for sure. Believe me, I've tried. I can't play a fiddle or a piano to save my life, trying to keep time on a drum confuses my brain, and as for singing...well, let's just say that I'm happy to let the rest of them handle the vocals. The boring truth is that I play the guitar. My parents shoved it at me because they needed me to do *something*, and for years I've stood behind them all onstage, strumming away like some kind of an idiot.

Not to blow my own horn, but I'm actually pretty good. It's just that I don't really get to perform much. I mean, I play the whole time, but it's basically filler. I do a bit of finger picking, but mostly I just bang out the chords and keep the rhythm like a trained monkey backing up an orchestra. At one point or another, I've tried to learn pretty much every other instrument that might fit in with the rest of the noise onstage—mandolin, pipes, piano, even accordion—but none of them stuck. I just don't have the feel for things the way the rest of my family does, so I'm destined to stand behind them all, strumming my guitar and wishing I was somewhere else.

My lack of musical versatility isn't the only thing that sets me apart from my family. A few years ago a reporter for the tourism section of the *New York Times* did a story about Cape Breton Island, and we actually got a mention. "The Family McClintock is the real deal," the *Times* declared. "A family band in the truest sense of the word. Six children and their parents and all but one of them sporting pale skin dotted with freckles and the brightest red hair west of Scotland. When this rowdy crew gets going onstage, it's a sight to see. Absolutely not to be missed, especially for their dance routines."

"All but one of them" refers to me, indirectly. Neil, the middle child. Kathy's drop-dead beautiful, and in a few years the twins will look just like her. Shamus is tall and good-looking and has girls falling all over him. It's only a matter of time before Johnny has the same problem. He's younger than I am, but he's already a couple of inches taller. It's no wonder they stick me at the back of the stage. I'm the runty, pudgy, black-haired black sheep of the family, with a distinct lack of moves.

We haven't rehearsed in months, since Christmas vacation, so it's pretty impressive that things sound as tight as they do as quickly as they do. We start off with our classic intro piece, a fast, upbeat tune called "Off to the Dance" that gives everyone a chance to do their thing. The song builds in layers until everyone is part of the action. Shamus gets things going by thrumming out a steady rolling beat on his drum; then I come in with a simple repetitive chord sequence, A–D–G–A, that fills in the sound a bit and sets the stage. My mother is next, dropping into the action with a nice piano run that turns into a bright and cheerful melody line. Johnny and

Dad start at the same time, Dad on fiddle and Johnny on penny whistle. They go back and forth for a few bars, "Dueling Banjos" style, and then the girls dance out to the front, Kathy down the middle of the group and the twins on either side. They start dancing gracefully in perfect unison, and the music backs them up nicely as they side-kick and front-step and twirl back and forth across the concrete floor of the garage.

The music comes to a gentle lull, and the three girls curtsy neatly. The audience is meant to get the impression that the song has come to a close, but after a pregnant pause we kick into overdrive. I strum harder and start to do a bit of fast picking, Mom's piano really gets going, and Dad walks out in front with the fiddle and faces the girls, who begin an intricate stepdance routine. At first they dance together, then one at a time, so that it appears as if the music is moving across the floor through their feet, snapping from one to the next. Dad is something to see when he really gets into the music. He's crouching and playing as fast as they dance, and their feet and his bow are moving so quickly you can barely see them. Gradually the rest of us drop out of the song until it's just the fiddle and the feet, playing off one another. Finally, a crescendo of music and footsteps comes to a sudden end, and all of us take a dramatic stage bow, holding our instruments out to our sides and keeping still for a few seconds for the applause.

Obviously, there is no applause during practice, but we know to expect it. Our audiences love this stuff. If I'm being totally honest, I have to say I've never really liked the music we play, but, as my parents have pointed out to us over and over again, this gig is going to pay our way through university. Don't get me wrong. We aren't getting rich from doing this, but if we're lucky and the gigs keep coming, we might just end up with a debt-free start to life. Rock and roll.

Three

After running through a few more tunes, my dad gets my brothers and sisters to line up and start practicing the big dance centerpiece to the show. The routine is elaborate and involves a lot of back and forth between the boys and the girls. It would make sense for me to be included, since it would pair up three guys and three girls, but like I said, I'm not cut out for dancing. My parents did their best to teach me, but eventually they had to throw in the towel and admit that I wasn't a twinkletoes like the rest of the gang. That's why I just hang out in the background and strum away, a big fake smile plastered to my face.

"Are we done practicing after this?" I ask my mom.

"Yep," she says. "Why don't you go and keep your grandmother company? Scoot before your dad notices."

She doesn't need to tell me twice.

Gran's in the kitchen, kneading a massive lump of glossy brown dough for her famous porridge bread. There's a turkey in the oven, and the whole house smells amazing.

I grab a seat at the table and absentmindedly strum on my guitar.

"Where's the rest of the dog and pony show?" she asks.

"They're dancing," I tell her. I don't need to go into detail—everyone knows I've got two left feet.

"I guess they'll be twice as hungry when they come in," she says. "You'd better come over here and get a couple of these into you before the rest of them have a chance to gobble them up."

Her eyes twinkle as she slides a plate of her famous cranberry scones, still wafting steam, across the counter. I stand the guitar up against the table and come over to grab one.

"Yum," I say, breaking off a piece and sticking it into my mouth.

"There's butter in the fridge," she tells me.

"I like them like this," I say. There's nothing better than a warm scone straight out of the oven. Gran's the best cook in the world. Her specialty is old-school Scottish food—oatcakes, farm cheese, bread-and-butter pickles. Yes, she makes haggis, but it isn't nearly as bad as people seem to think. It's basically a giant sausage. If that grosses you out, you should show up sometime when she's making blood pudding. It's pretty much exactly what it sounds like, and it's delicious. My dad and I are the only ones who'll eat the stuff.

"Dancing aside, how was practice?" asks Gran. She's forming loaves, putting them into pans and covering them with tea towels to rise.

"Same same," I say, stuffing a second scone into my mouth.

She smiles at me, shaking her head. "I don't know how you people do it," she says. "When your parents told me that they were thinking of putting you all onstage, I didn't believe it. I definitely didn't think it would last this long. Now look at you."

"Yeah, lucky us," I say.

"Well, you can pick your friends and you can pick your nose, but you can't pick your family," she says. "As long as you're stuck with them, you might as well make nice music together."

"Stuck is a good way to put it," I say.

"How do you think I feel?" she asks. "I'm not gonna graduate from high school in a few years with my whole life out there waiting for me. I'm here in the zoo for the long haul, or at least until they put me on an ice floe and push me out to sea."

"I never thought about that, Gran," I say. "Maybe we should start making plans to escape."

"Save up those music bucks, boy. We'll go online and buy a secondhand motorcycle with a sidecar and then hit the road for Argentina. You can teach yourself gaucho music, and I'll find some wealthy retiree with a cattle farm who's looking for a nice Canadian lady to settle down with."

"I didn't realize you were in the market, Gran."

"The only reason I haven't remarried is because all the eligible bachelors in this town are widowers, and I was friends or enemies with every single one of their wives. I can't stand the thought of them gossiping about me up in heaven. Or wherever they are."

I'm still laughing when the rest of the family comes tumbling into the kitchen, all of them talking over each other.

"Who's hungry?" asks Gran.

Stupid question. Just as she predicted, the scones are gone in about ten seconds flat.

"Everyone listen up for a minute," yells Mom. "I need you all to give me a list of your current measurements so I can get our stagewear finalized."

We begin calling out our sizes at her, but she holds up her hand and pulls a piece of paper and a pen from a drawer. "Write it all down," she says, handing the paper to Shamus. "I'm not a dictation machine."

Supper is typically delicious. Gran's gone overboard, and the table is packed with food. You'd think it was Christmas.

"So are you going to fill us in on why we barely heard from you this semester, Kathy?" asks Dad.

"You heard from me," she says.

"Once a week, if we were lucky," says Mom.

"Once a week is a lot, Mom. How much did you want me to call? I told you, school was really busy.

I had a big research project that I worked on for almost three months."

"The kind of research project that makes you blush," says Shamus, and he's right. Her face is beet red. Kathy can't hide anything. None of the rest of them can either. One of the advantages of my darker complexion is that I don't look like I'm going to cry or freak out every ten minutes.

"Is there a guy?" I ask her.

"You could say that," she says. "His name is Casey."

"Weird name," say Maura and Molly at the same time.

"Not really," says Kathy.

"Is he the reason you were late coming home this year?" asks Johnny.

"Pretty much," she says. "He needed help with a project he's been working on, so I stuck around for a few weeks to give him a hand. Anyway, he's gone."

"What do you mean?" asks Gran.

"I mean he graduated a couple of weeks ago. I was helping him tie up some loose ends, but he's gone to Africa to do development work."

"For good?" asks Dad.

"For a few years, anyway," says Kathy.

"Well, I'm sorry to hear that, Kathy," says Mom.

"It's okay," says Kathy, although she doesn't look okay. "How's Delia?" she asks, turning to Shamus and changing the subject.

"He doesn't go out with Delia anymore," Maura says.

"Oh no," says Kathy.

"I'm going out with Mary Sexton," says Shamus.

"I thought you were dating Laureen Shea," says Mom.

"That was before Mary but after Delia," says Johnny.

"Wow, Shamus," says Kathy. "You've been busy."

"Listen up, guys," says Dad. "I think we need to talk about scheduling. We have a lot of shows booked for the next couple of months, and I expect we'll have more soon. It's important that we're all on the same page."

Scheduling. Ugh. The worst thing about being part of the Family McClintock is listening to Dad drone on about schedules. He goes into great detail about what shows we'll be playing, the acoustics of the venues, the types of audiences to expect, blah, blah, blah. None of it matters, as we don't remember any of this crap and we always put on the same show, more or less.

Gran gets up and starts clearing plates as the rest of us try not to fall asleep.

I'm in the middle of doing this thing where I shift my eyes and the pattern in the tablecloth turns 3-D, when Dad says something that snaps me back to attention.

"But the real big news of the summer," he says, leaning back in his chair and looking at us with a gleam in his eye, "is that we are currently lined up to open for the Vince Beach Band in Halifax at the end of the month. Saturday after Deep Cove Days, if I remember correctly."

Our mouths drop open at the same time.

"What's the Vince Beach Band?" asks Gran, dropping pieces of pie in front of the twins.

"Are you kidding?" asks Johnny. "The Vince Beach Band is one of the biggest country bands of the last few years. You know, Gran—he sings 'Big Old Boots'."

"Never heard of him," she says.

"How the hell did you swing that, Dad?" asks Shamus as Molly and Maura start singing.

"Big old boots, big old hat, big old truck, ain't nothin' better than that."

"Turns out I used to go to school with one of his managers," says Dad. "I reconnected with him online a few months ago, and one thing led to another."

"We'll have a big old time at the bingo hall, I've got a big old heart, and you can have it all."

I'm not into country music, not even a little bit, but I have to admit that opening for the Vince Beach Band is a pretty big deal.

"We're not the only openers. It's a big show and they'll have a couple of other acts, but we'll get to do three songs," Dad says. He's obviously pleased with himself, and for good reason.

"That'll be a big audience," says Kathy.

"Biggest one we've played yet," says Mom. "By a long shot."

"Who knows, kids." says Dad. "This could be our leg up to the big leagues."

Four

"The Vince Beach Band?" asks Bert, his mouth hanging open.

"That's what I said," I tell him. We're back in his basement, trying to figure out what to play at the talent show. I've agreed to do it on two conditions: that he promises to practice, and that I can decide to pull out at the last minute if I want to.

I'm actually kind of excited now that I've decided to give it a shot. Bert's right. It can't hurt to put some effort into playing something I like for a change. Even if it all falls apart, it'll be kind of fun to jam without my parents breathing down my neck and my little sisters stepdancing around the room.

"That's totally nuts, Neil," he says. "The Vince Beach Band is, like, a real band! They're, like, on TV and in magazines and stuff."

"Yeah, Bert," I say. "I know."

"Wow," he says, shaking his head. "How does something like this even happen?"

"It's not that big a deal," I say. "Dad is friends with some guy who hooked us up."

"Oh man," says Bert. "You'll be rolling in cowgirls. Vince Beach kind of sucks, but chicks dig him. He's bound to let you make out with some of his extra honeys."

I laugh. "We'll see."

"So when is this happening, anyway?" he asks me.

"Saturday after Deep Cove Days," I tell him.

"You're sure it's not going to mess with the talent show?" he asks.

"Yes, Bert," I say. "It's on Saturday night, and I've told you a million times, we always have Thursday off."

A couple of years ago, when we found ourselves playing lots of shows, our parents laid down the rule that Thursday would always be a day off.

No practice, no shows, not even costume fittings or choreography. They said it was important for us to have a break to look forward to, and since a lot of our bookings are for Friday and Saturday nights, Thursday became our mini-weekend.

"So what's the plan, anyway?" I ask him. "Do we want to try to figure out a cover song, put our own spin on it?"

"No way, man," he says. "If we want to impress the judges, we need to show up with our own material."

He jumps up from his drum set and runs across the room to grab a pile of loose leaf, which he shoves at me.

"I've been working on some lyrics," he says. "I've got a couple of options. What do you think?"

I look at the first sheet. *Like Yo Wiggle* is written across the top in giant block letters, flanked by what I think are supposed to be naked women, but which look more like otters with wigs and big boobs.

"What is this?" I ask him.

"Just read it," he says.

I like yo wiggle.
I like yo jiggle.
Come on and snuggle,
My sexy muggle.

I look up from the paper. "*Sexy muggle?*"

He shrugs. "It's hard to find something that rhymes with '*snuggle*.'"

I shake my head and keep reading.

I wanna kiss ya.
I really miss ya.
I wanna make ya
A sexy cake, yeah.

"Bert, these are the worst lyrics I've ever heard," I say.

"Oh, well, excuse me," he says. "Maybe I should have written them in Gaelic, so you could truly appreciate them."

"Seriously, man, they're just rhyming couplets."

"What's wrong with couplets?" he asks. "The Beatles had lots of songs with quick, snappy rhymes."

"So you want us to be like the Beatles?"

"Not exactly," he says. "I was thinking of something more like Jay-Z meets One Direction, only with lots of hardcore drumming."

"Sorry, Bert, it sucks," I say. "There's not even a chorus."

"Fine," he says, snatching it away from me. "Read the other one."

He's obviously taken more time with this one. Half of the words have been scratched out and rewritten.

Pass the Test

I really hate to study, but I'd study lots for you.
I'd listen well, so you could tell that I'm in love with you.
I'd work hard on my essays, my readings would get read
And I'd go over all your lessons, every night in bed.

Chorus:
I wanna pass the test.
I want you to be impressed.
Out of all your other students,
I want you to like me best.

"Holy crap, Bert," I say, looking up. "This isn't half bad."

"You think so?" he asks.

"Well, it has a chorus at least," I tell him. I keep reading.

I'll meet you in your classroom, when everyone's
gone home,
And you can give me special lessons, now that
we're alone.
If I can be your favorite, the apple of your eye
I'll write it on the chalkboard, a hundred
thousand times.

I wish that graduation wasn't quite so far away,
I wish that I could kiss you on your luscious
lips today,
I wish that you were thirty, and I was twenty-nine,
I wish that you weren't married to that meathead
Mr. Klein.

"Bert!" I say. "This song is about Mrs. Klein?" Mrs. Klein is our math teacher. Bert is always talking about how hot she is, but personally, I find her kind of scary.

"I think I love her," he says. "She's so hot."

"You are insane," I tell him. "We can't use this song. We'll get in trouble."

"Leave that to me," he says. "All I have to do is rewrite the last verse and nobody will have any idea who the song is about."

"I guess that could work," I say. "I have to admit, the lyrics are pretty catchy."

"What about music?" he says. "Do you have anything in your bag of tricks?"

Although I like to make up melodies and screw around with different chord progressions, I've never tried to do anything with lyrics. I try out a few riffs I've messed around with, but we both agree that none of them sound right.

"I don't know," I say. "I guess we have to start with one or the other. Trying to combine lyrics that have already been written with music that's already been written just doesn't work."

"Well, we have the lyrics," he says.

"Yeah. Give me some time to come up with something," I tell him. "I still don't know how we're going to make this work without a singer, though."

"We'll find one," he says. "You've gotta have faith, my man. I think we should start asking around, see if anyone's interested."

"Yeah, well, don't blab it everywhere yet," I tell him. "I don't want anyone in my family to find out that I'm doing this."

"What's the big deal?" he asks. "You guys play music for a living. What difference does it make if you have a little side thing going on?"

"I just don't want anyone interfering," I tell him.

"Whatever you say, man," he says. "But I sure wouldn't mind some help from Kathy."

I spend a little time trying to come up with some music for the song, but nothing comes to me. When Bert starts banging around on his drums, suggesting that he might find a melody in the noise, I decide to leave. I'll probably have an easier time figuring something out with a clear head.

Five

On the first Saturday of July, we cram into the minibus and head off for our first show of the season.

My parents bought the bus a couple of years ago, when we started getting more out-of-county bookings. It originally belonged to the Nova Scotia Department of Natural Resources. It's old and kind of beat-up, with some rust around the wheel wells, but it runs well and, like Dad always says, as long as it gets us to our shows on time, it doesn't need to be pretty. It's still its original bold blue, although Dad has painted over the government logo and stenciled the band name on the back and sides. It's safe to say that we stick out when we're on the road. The most important thing is that it fits all of us.

There's room for twelve passengers, all of our gear and some boxes of the swag that Gran sells at the merchandise table before and after our shows.

Today's gig isn't far from Deep Cove. We drive just a few miles out of town and then Dad turns on to an unpaved road, and we chug along for a few hundred meters before pulling into a gravel parking lot behind a quaint old church. We've done this same show, a fundraiser for the church, every year since we started performing. It's a good way to kick off the season. The acoustics are great, the crowd is small but enthusiastic, and, best of all, the local ladies make sure we're well fed. There's always a table full of sweets and little sandwiches set up in the meeting room at the back of the building. It's kind of like a green room, only there's a picture of Jesus staring down at us while we eat.

Johnny and I help Shamus and Kathy unload the gear from the bus while Mom and Dad go inside to find Gladys, the woman responsible for organizing the event. Gran drags the merch boxes out and starts to organize them, and the twins chase Gladys's dog, Buster, into the field behind the church.

"In here, guys," Dad calls from the front of the church as Johnny and I hustle one of our amps through the back door. We maneuver around the tables and chairs in the meeting room and make our way out front. We stomp up some steps and onto a wooden stage that faces the pews, and set down the amp. The thud echoes through the church.

"Hello, boys," says Gladys. "Glad you could make it again this year."

She's staring at me with an eyebrow raised, and I wonder if I have a booger hanging out of my nose. Then I notice my Dad pointing at his head.

"Oh, right," I say, reaching up to pull off my baseball cap.

Gladys smiles and turns back to my parents. "What a lovely bunch of children you have. To think of all that talent under one roof. It must be just wonderful, all of you living together and making music."

"Wonderful" isn't exactly the word I would have chosen.

I help Gran set up a folding table by the front door and carry the T-shirts and CDs in for her, then head back to the meeting room to check out the grub.

Shamus and Kathy have carted the last of the instruments in from the bus and are taking them out of the cases. I grab my guitar and drag a chair over beside the food table. I shove a couple of cookies into my mouth and begin to pick away on my guitar.

From the front of the church, I hear my mother begin to run chords along the piano. It sounds pretty flat, but Mom has yet to meet a warped old piano that she can't wrestle a tune out of. Sure enough, she quickly gets a feel for it, and as she starts to play a little jig, the noise magically turns into music.

I quietly strum on the guitar, listening to her play and twisting the tuning pegs until the guitar is in tune with piano. We always tune from the piano. Usually, Mom just plugs in her electric keyboard, which makes things pretty easy, but when she has the chance to play on a big old-fashioned upright like the one in this church, she can't resist if it's even halfway playable.

Once I get my guitar tuned to the piano, I begin to play along with what she's doing. I chord at first, then add a bit of finger picking, working off the notes she's playing so that a bit of harmony emerges. This is what happens when we're all onstage—our instruments start speaking to one another.

People march in and out of the meeting room, moving instruments, dragging cables, discussing acoustics and space for dancing. Nobody pays any attention to me, which is how I like it.

Mom stops playing abruptly, and I hear her discussing something with Dad. I reach over and grab a sandwich. While I'm chewing, I run through Bert's lyrics in my head.

I've been thinking about them for the past couple of days, trying to come up with a melody line. Playing along with my mother seems to have unstuck something. I start to pick out a tune on the guitar, starting and stopping, gradually figuring out what will work, what will sound good but also be unique.

The twins come running in from outside, breathless and sweaty, their hair a mess. They skip over to the food table.

"What are you doing?" Molly asks.

"Thinking about Vince Beach," I say. "He's so dreeeeeamy."

They both giggle and run off with some cookies.

I go through the lyrics in my head one more time, strumming absentmindedly, and suddenly the tune drops into place as if it's been there all along. I almost laugh at how easy it seems now that I've got it figured out, even though I couldn't for the life of me tell you where it came from. I strum and pick faster, humming along with the guitar. I want to be sure I commit the melody to memory before I get distracted and lose it forever.

My father sticks his head into the room. "Neil! Quit goofing around and help your brother run cables up to the speakers in the balcony. We'll be playing in less than an hour. Get a move on!"

"You got it," I say, jumping up from my chair. I'm still hanging on to my guitar, and I quickly run through the melody line one more time before I place it carefully into its case. Then I grab a couple of brownies and head out front to help.

* * *

The show goes well. There are definitely more people here than last year. The pews are so full that some people have to stand around the edges. Dad's been saying for a couple of years now that as word spreads, we'll become more and more in demand. Looking out at today's audience, I get the feeling he's right.

For one thing, the average age of the audience seems to have dropped by quite a bit. The old ladies who've flocked to our past performances are still here, soaking it up, but there are also quite a few young people in their twenties and thirties, many of them with little kids. I'm not surprised that the audience is almost entirely devoid of teenagers, but there is one notable exception. She's around my age, and I've never seen her before. She's got short black hair and glasses with bright red frames, and she's wearing jean shorts and a plain white tank top. She's sitting in the front row with an old lady and a little boy who keeps fidgeting. The old lady is so engrossed in the music that she doesn't pay any attention to the kid, but the girl manages to keep him under control. Every once in a while she leans in and whispers something in his ear, and he laughs and calms down.

My best guess is that the old lady is their grandmother, and red-glasses girl has been dragged along to the show to babysit. She's pretty cute, and throughout the show I keep stealing glances at her, hoping nobody catches on. I'm not too worried. The chance of anyone paying attention to me while the rest of the McClintock circus sings, dances and plays weird instruments is pretty slim.

Afternoon shows are usually a bit more subdued than nighttime performances, especially when they're at churches or community centers. Something about the surprising energy of today's crowd gets us going, though, and by the fourth tune we're really pumping out a good set. Even though I am not a fan of the music, I have to admit that it's pretty cool when a show goes especially well. We're always well rehearsed enough to sound good at any performance, but every once in a while we're on fire, and today is one of those days.

Without even noticing, I start to really get into what we're playing. The piano and fiddle are pounding away, and the twins are at center stage, facing each other and doing a dance-off. For little girls, they sure can move. They play to the audience, throwing in some hand gestures and occasionally snapping their heads sideways and winking to the crowd at the exact same moment. People go nuts for the mirror-image stuff.

I take advantage of the audience's focus on them to glance at red-glasses girl and realize with a shock that she's looking right at me. I immediately drop my eyes, but when I peek again, she's still staring, only now she's smiling at me. I'm so surprised that I miss a few chords. I catch the tune again almost immediately, hoping nobody will notice, but something tells me it didn't slip by my dad.

Six

After the show, we bring our instruments into the back room and put them safely away before heading back out to mingle with the crowd. I hate this part of the job more than anything. I'm no good at small talk, and it takes some serious effort to pretend that I'm in love with Celtic music.

Of all of us, Shamus and Kathy are best at the schmoozing thing, probably because they're older and have had more practice. The twins just stick close to Mom and smile and giggle at everyone, which, of course, people love. At least Johnny hates the meet-and-greet as much as I do. Dad won't let us skip it, though, so we usually stick together as far away from the crowd as possible.

"What is up with all the hipster families?" I ask him when we're standing off to the side.

"I know, right?" he says. "I guess Dad's onto something when he talks about us catching the wave."

"What wave?" I ask.

"Are you serious?" says Johnny. "He's always going on about how Celtic music is coming up, and we're totally in the right place at the right time. Do you ever bother to listen to him?"

"Not really," I say. "He talks too much. I just hop on the bus when everyone else does."

He laughs. "I should try that." He glances past me. "Incoming."

I turn around in time to see the old lady from the front row hurrying up to us, clutching her program in her hands. Red-glasses girl and the little kid are following her.

"Oh my goodness!" says the lady. "I can't tell you how much I enjoyed that show."

"Thanks," Johnny and I say simultaneously.

"Honestly," she says. "I grew up in Cape Breton, and I was transported right back to my childhood. How wonderful that you're all keeping it alive, and in such fine fashion!"

We get a lot of this kind of nostalgic enthusiasm at our shows, from people who grew up here or who had parents who grew up here or who've always been fans of traditional fiddle music and *just had to come hear it for themselves.*

"Thanks," I say again. "I'm glad you liked it."

She looks past me at Johnny. "You know," she says, "I always wanted to play the bagpipes. Do you think it's too late for me to pick it up?"

I slide out of the way and leave Johnny to give her a pep talk. Red-glasses girl smiles at me and holds out her hand.

"Hey," she says. "I'm Sandy."

I shake her hand. "I'm Neil."

"I know," she says. "Your name is in the program. This is Beast." The kid makes claws with his hands and growls at me.

"Beast," I say. "That's a pretty wild name."

Sandy leans in as if she's about to let me in on something big. "His name isn't really Beast," she says in a mock whisper. "It's Bailey. He only answers to Beast these days, though."

I look at the kid, who narrows his eyes at me and emits a low snarl.

"I can see why," I say. "So are you guys around for a while?"

"Grandma's rented a cottage for the month," she says. "We're here until just after Deep Cove Days. Then we head back home to Toronto."

"Cool," I say. This is the part where any clear-headed red-blooded teenage dude would ask if she wants to hang out sometime, but of course I can only come up with "cool."

"You guys were really good," she says.

"Oh yeah?" I ask. "This your kind of thing?"

She leans in again. "To tell you the truth, I'm not really into Celtic music."

I laugh. "To tell *you* the truth, neither am I."

"I'm serious though," she says. "I was totally digging your playing. You're really good."

"You think so?" I ask, thanking my DNA for the millionth time that I don't blush like the rest of the clan.

"Totally," she says. "I actually play a little bit myself."

"No way," I say. "That's really cool."

"Sandy!" says Beast, reaching up and grabbing her shirt. "When are we going?"

Their grandmother, who's been grilling Johnny, turns around.

"I suppose you're right, Bailey," she says. "We should start thinking about what we're going to pick up for the barbecue tonight."

"It was cool to meet you," I manage to say to Sandy. Apparently the only word I know how to use is "cool." My brain is spinning and I'm trying to figure out how to ask if she wants to jam sometime, when she saves me the trouble.

"We should get together and play guitar sometime," she says. "If you're interested. I don't really know anyone around here."

"Yeah," I manage to spit out. "Sounds great."

We exchange numbers, and Johnny and I watch as they walk away.

"You definitely got the better side of that deal," he says. "You've got a date with a cute girl, and I think I might have agreed to give bagpipe lessons to an old lady."

* * *

In the bus, everyone is excited about how well the show went.

"It was tight, guys," says Dad. "Really, really tight. The only time I heard anything screwy was when Neil dropped out for a few bars about halfway through 'Fisherman's Reel'." He twists the rearview mirror until he can see me, sitting way at the back.

"Yeah," I grunt. "Sorry." Of course he has to finish off his praise of the show with a dig at me.

"No big deal, guy," he says. "But maybe you and I should sit down over the next couple of days and work through your parts. Don't want you to get left behind."

It hadn't sounded all that bad to me.

"I think everyone sounded perfect," says Gran. "I had half a mind to jump up there on stage and throw a few steps down myself." She leans over the seat in front of her, where Molly and Maura are sitting. "What do you think, girls? Should old Gran get some new dance shoes and join the show?"

The twins are giggling at her as we pull in to our driveway.

"How did it feel being back onstage, Kathy?" Dad asks as we're unloading the bus.

"It was good," she says. She must realize how unenthusiastic she sounds, because she forces a smile and adds, "It was great. I really missed it.

48

Sorry—I guess I'm kind of tired. Is it okay if I go take a nap?"

"Of course," says Mom.

Kathy disappears into the house, and I see Mom and Dad exchange a look.

"She's acting very strange," says Dad.

"She's heartbroken," says Mom. "I think she really likes this guy, and now to have him move to the other side of the world...We should all give her a bit of space."

"She should brush it off and find someone new," says Shamus. "Moping over him isn't going to do her any good."

"Listen to you, Casanova," says Gran. "We can't all find a new soul mate every week and a half."

"I'm just saying that if I was going out with some chick and she moved away to China or Argentina or someplace, I wouldn't lose sleep over it," he says.

"You should write Valentine's cards, Shamus," says Johnny.

We hustle the last of the equipment into the garage, and Dad shuts and locks the door.

"Great first show, gang," he says. "Now let's see if we can keep that up all summer."

Seven

I n the morning, Dad herds us into the garage and we spend a couple of hours running through our newer songs. He tells us to break early, but before I have a chance to escape with everyone else, he asks me to stay.

"Why don't we take a crack at some of your stuff?" he says. "Work the kinks out."

"I guess so," I say. "I didn't realize there were any kinks."

"Nothing serious," he says. "I've just noticed that you seem to be drifting off a bit during practice. Almost like you might not be putting everything into it."

I know he's right. I've been daydreaming lately, uninterested in the stuff I'm expected to play. It's just so boring to do the same backup on the same songs, one performance after the other. I don't really understand what the big deal is— it's not like anyone comes to the shows to see me. I know how far that argument will get me, though, so I grab a stool to sit across from him.

"So I've noticed that you've been getting a bit lazy," he says. "You're falling back on chords too often. Let's try 'Old Joe's on the Town Tonight.' I'll take you up to the bridge, then you play through it for me."

He drops right into the song without even thinking about it. He can be a bit of a slave driver, but I have to admit that my old man is a hell of a talented musician. I listen for the melody line, tapping out the rhythm against my guitar, and pick it up when he hits the bridge. He's right that I've been cheating through this part for a while now, relying on chords instead of picking out the tune, which is more difficult, so when I try to do it the way I originally learned it, I screw it up.

He puts his hand up. "Okay, hang on," he says. "See what happens when you get lazy for a few shows? You lose it."

"Dad, I don't get what the big deal is," I say. "It sounds fine when I just keep the rhythm."

"Well, we don't want it to sound fine," he says. "We want it to sound great. Neil, you know how this works. We're only as good as our weakest part. I know you're better than this. I've heard you play these songs a thousand times."

"Nobody is coming out to see me," I protest.

"You're right," he says. "They're coming to see all of us. Together. Now, I want you to run through this piece with me until we've got it down pat."

I resist the urge to roll my eyes.

We run through "Old Joe's" a few more times, and then he makes me practice two more songs until he's satisfied. By the time we start to get rolling, I'm half glad he forced me to do it. Sometimes I have to remind myself that I probably wouldn't know how to play guitar at all if it wasn't for my semi-famous family.

We're at it for more than an hour. "Okay," he says finally. "That's good for today. How do you feel about it?"

"Good," I admit. "I think it'll sound better now."

"You're darn right," he says.

"I was wondering something," I say. "I've been thinking about 'Off to the Dance' and wondering if maybe I could come up with a solo."

"Oh yeah?" he asks skeptically.

"It doesn't have to be a big deal," I tell him. "I kind of have something worked out."

"Let's hear it," he says, sitting back down.

"Okay," I say. "So it's right after Shamus comes in with the bodhran. I was thinking we could add a few bars, and I could play against the drum for a bit."

He nods and listens as I push out the riff I've been working on in the back of my head since last summer.

"Something like that," I say when I'm done.

"I like it, Neil," he says. "I'm glad you're thinking about the music this seriously. I'm not sure it'll work with the tune the way we have it arranged, but keep working on your own ideas. Who knows, maybe you'll even end up writing your own songs someday."

Figures, I think, as I walk back to the house. He's got no problem telling us what to do, day in and day out, but the minute I come up with a small suggestion, he rules it out without even thinking about it.

I grab some cookies and a can of soda and head down to my bedroom in the basement.

I lie on my bed and strum my guitar for a few minutes, then sit up and grab my phone.

I scroll through my contacts and find Sandy's name. Then, without giving myself a chance to lose my nerve, I call her.

The phone rings a couple of times before someone picks up. I hear breathing on the other end of the line, but nobody says anything.

"Hello?" I say.

"ROOOOOAAAAARRRRRR," someone screams, so loudly that I almost drop my phone. I hold it away from my head until the screaming has stopped, then listen again.

"Oh my god, Bailey," I hear someone say. "What is wrong with you?" Then, into the phone: "Hello?"

It's her. "Hi, Sandy?"

"Yes, who's this?"

"It's Neil McClintock. Uh, from, uh, the Family McClintock." It comes out sounding so completely ridiculous that I want to crawl under my bed.

"Oh, Neil! Hey!" she says. "I'm so sorry about the hollering. I try to keep Beast away from my phone, but he's just too quick. So how's it going?"

"It's going good," I say. "I was wondering if you were still interested in maybe getting together to jam sometime."

"Totally," she says. "I'm dying to hang out with someone who isn't a monster child or a senior citizen. When were you thinking?"

"Uh, I don't know," I say. I haven't thought that far ahead.

"What are you doing now?" she asks. "Can you get a ride to our cottage?"

"I'll have to see if anyone is around to take me," I say. "I'll let you know as soon as I check."

"Sounds good," she says. "I'll text you directions."

This has turned out to be a lot easier than I expected. I run upstairs to look for a ride, but nobody is around.

I finally find Gran in the garden. "Where are Mom and Dad?" I ask.

"They just headed out to run some errands," she says. "They'll be home for supper."

"What about Shamus?"

"I think he's out somewhere with whatever girl he's dating these days."

"Oh sh—"

"Language," she warns.

"Shoot," I say. "I really need a ride somewhere."

"I think Kathy's in her room," says Gran. "Maybe she'll drive you in the bus."

"Sure," says Kathy when I ask her. "I could stand to think about something else for a while."

It's always weird to be driving in the bus when it's not full of people. I try not to think about global warming and promise myself that I'll buy some carbon credits if I actually score with Sandy.

"So who am I taking you to see?" Kathy asks as we bump along the unpaved road to Sandy's cottage.

"Some girl I met at the church show yesterday," I tell her.

"Oooh," she says. "A girl. Should I be intrigued?"

"You can be as intrigued as you want. Just don't mention it to anyone," I say.

"Don't worry," she says. "I know all about trying to keep secrets in this family."

"What's going on with you, anyway?" I ask. "Are you upset about that guy?"

She sighs. "Yeah. I keep thinking about next year, and what's going to happen."

"What do you mean?"

She glances over at me. She seems to be contemplating something. "Can you keep a secret?" she asks finally.

"Yeah," I say. "For sure."

"There's a program I'm looking into. It's offered through the university, and it would let me get credit for doing some international development work. I could probably arrange to work on the project that Casey is managing, in Senegal."

"That would be cool," I say.

"The thing is, it would begin immediately after I finish my next year of school. Which would mean I'd be leaving in late April or early May, and I'd be gone until September."

"What about the band?" I ask.

"Exactly," she says. "I don't know what to do. If I don't come home next year, a lot of things will change."

"Do Mom and Dad know?"

"No," she says. "I know I can't leave it too much longer, but I can't figure out how to tell them. You know what Dad is like."

"Yep," I say. "That's pretty crazy, Kathy."

"You said it." She slows down. "Is this the place?"

I spot a number painted on a piece of driftwood at the end of the driveway and check it against the address I put in my phone. "Looks like it," I say. "Just drop me off here and I'll walk the rest of the way. Thanks for the ride. I promise I won't say anything."

She smiles. "I know you won't. Don't worry—everything will work out. Now get out of here. Go have some fun."

I grab my guitar from behind my seat and hop out, slapping the side of the bus as she drives away.

The driveway is steep, and I'm huffing and puffing by the time I reach the cottage. I'd like to take a minute to catch my breath before I knock on the door, but Sandy is sitting on the front deck, strumming her guitar, and sees me before I have the chance. She props her guitar in her chair and comes over to greet me.

"You want something to drink?" she asks. "Grandma took Beast to the beach."

I set my guitar on the deck and follow her inside. The cottage is a typical summer rental—

beat-up old furniture, some faded prints on the wall and a stack of well-used board games on top of a shelf full of paperback novels. Sandy pours us juice, and we take it out to the deck.

"It's nice here," I say. The cottage looks out on hills and trees. We can glimpse a narrow strip of ocean in the distance.

"Yeah," she says. "It's okay. It's a bit isolated. I have to ask Grandma to drive me any time I want to go anywhere."

"I know what that's like," I tell her. "So what were you playing before I showed up?"

"Oh." She glances at her guitar. "It wasn't anything serious. I was just fooling around."

"You should play something for me," I say.

"Can we maybe try doing something together?" she asks. "I'm a little shy to play in front of a professional musician."

"Give me a break," I say, laughing. "Sure, let's do it."

We mess around for a while, playing some oldies that we both know, like "American Pie" and "Harvest Moon." She only plays chords, but she's pretty good. When her shyness wears off a bit and we start to get into it, she begins to sing.

Her voice is husky and sweet, and when she really gets into a song, she closes her eyes and throws her head back. I could listen to—and watch—her all day.

By the time her grandmother and Beast get back from the beach, I've lost track of time. Beast runs growling onto the deck, wearing a baseball cap with seaweed hanging from it.

"What happened to you?" asks Sandy.

"I'm a sea beast!" he yells, running into the cottage.

"Hello, Neil," says Sandy's grandmother. "I'm glad you were able to come keep Sandy company."

"It was fun," I say. "But I should probably call home and get someone to come pick me up."

"Don't be silly," says her grandmother. "I'll drive you. Sandy, can you make sure Bailey takes a shower? I'll start getting supper ready when I get home."

"Let me know next time you're free and want to hang out," says Sandy as I'm getting into the car. "I'd really like to jam again soon, if you're up for it."

"Definitely," I say. "It was fun."

In the car, I try to politely answer her grandmother's many questions about "the musical life," but I'm dying to text Bert. As soon as she drops me off and drives away, I pull my phone out of my pocket.

How do you feel about a girl singer? I type.

Eight

B ert doesn't take much convincing. That a
cute girl might actually be willing to hang
out with us, even if it's just for practice, is
more than enough reason to give it a try as far as
he's concerned.

Sandy, on the other hand, is a tougher sell.

"I don't think I'm good enough," she says
when I call to ask her about it.

"You are!" I say. "You have a great voice, and
you can play rhythm guitar too. It'll be fun!"

"I don't know," she says. "What if I look stupid?"

"Trust me," I say. "Next to Bert, you and I
will look like we should be performing at the
Grammys. At least come to one practice before
you decide."

"Okay," she finally agrees. "But I'm not making any promises."

When I arrive at Bert's house for our first full band practice, I'm shocked to find that he's actually cleaned his basement. Not only has the garbage everywhere been picked up, but the floor has been vacuumed, his clothes are put away, and there's even a lit candle in the bathroom.

"What?" he says when he sees me looking around the room with my mouth hanging open. "This is the first time I've ever had a girl down here. I don't want her to think I'm a total slob."

"I'm impressed," I say.

"It's like you think I'm a Neanderthal or something," he says, then belches dramatically. We both bust up laughing.

The door at the top of the stairs opens, and his mom calls down, "Knock knock! You have company!"

Sandy comes down the stairs, her guitar slung over her shoulder and Beast clomping after her.

"Sorry," she says. "I promised I'd babysit him before we set this up."

Bert and Beast regard each other warily.

"You play video games?" asks Bert.

Beast lets out an affirmative grunt, and Bert gets him set up in front of the TV with a pair of headphones.

"So," says Sandy. "What's the plan? What are we playing?"

Bert and I hand her the lyrics to "Pass the Test" and do a slowed-down run-through the song. I'm impressed with Bert. Not only has he rewritten the final verse, he's also done a lot of practicing on his drums. I've been working on the guitar parts, too, and I find that I'm really happy with the way it's coming together.

Sandy nods along as we play, her eyes on the page of lyrics. "Cool," she says when we're finished. "I like it."

"You want to try singing?" I ask.

"I think I'd prefer to play along a few times first," she says. "Just to get comfortable."

"Anything we can do to make you comfortable," says Bert suggestively. I shoot him a dirty look, but she's getting her guitar out of her case and doesn't seem to notice.

We spend the next hour or so going over the song. It's more barebones than I'm used to, just two guitars and drums, but it sounds pretty good, despite the occasional unnerving bellow or roar from Beast, who's focused on the TV. After five run-throughs, Sandy finally starts to sing, and that's when things really fall into place.

"That sounded great!" says Bert when we've finished.

"How did it feel?" I ask her.

"Felt good," she says. "It was fun. It's a cool song."

"It sounded good," I agree. "But I'm not sure about the way you sing the second half of the chorus."

"Okay," she says. "So how should I sing it?"

"Yeah, Neil," says Bert. "She isn't a mind reader."

I hate singing, but I try to show her what I mean. "*Out of all your other students, I want you to like me best*," I sing, feeling totally self-conscious.

"I don't know why you're always going on about not being able to sing," says Bert.

"Yeah," says Sandy. "You've got a nice voice."

"Whatever," I say. "Do you guys want to run through it again?"

We play through the song a few more times, and when Sandy's grandmother arrives to pick her and Beast up, we're sounding really tight.

"So you're in?" I ask Sandy as she packs up her guitar.

"Yeah," she says, turning around and smiling at us. "I think it'll be fun."

"Perfect," says Bert. "There's just one more thing to figure out. What are we going to call ourselves?"

"We only have one song," I say. "Do we really need a name?"

"Are you crazy?" he asks. "Nobody is going to take us seriously without a name. Besides, we only have one song because it's our first song. The Stones, U2, Arcade Fire—they all *only* had one song once too."

"He's got a point," says Sandy.

We stand at the foot of the stairs, mulling it over for a minute. A horn honks outside, for the third time. "How about we all think about it and see what we come up with," says Sandy. "Beast and I better get out of here before Grandma has a fit."

"I've got to hand it to you, Neil," says Bert, once Sandy has wrangled Beast and her guitar up the stairs. "She is exactly what this band has been looking for."

Nine

The Family McClintock has never been busier. Dad has us rehearsing like crazy for the Vince Beach show, and we're also getting plenty of other bookings. Some days we wake up, eat a big breakfast and then head to the garage to rehearse before getting in the bus and driving several hours to a show, only to crawl into bed exhausted at the end of a long day and then wake up and do it all over again.

Somehow I manage to find time to practice with Sandy and Bert, squeezing in an hour or two here and there on days when we don't have performances scheduled. I especially look forward to Thursdays, which I'm able to spend entirely in Bert's basement. Beast is usually around for our practices, too, and has kind of become our unofficial mascot.

Now that "Pass the Test" is pretty tight, we start to play some cover tunes, mostly for fun but also because Sandy makes the good point that we should have an encore ready in case we win the talent show. Soon we have a solid repertoire of three songs: one original and two covers.

The funny thing is, the more I get to work on the stuff I like with Sandy and Bert, the more my guitar playing seems to improve when I'm onstage with my family. My parents notice too.

"You were on fire tonight, Neil," my mom says one night. We're on the highway, coming home from a traditional music festival in New Brunswick.

"I just played my parts," I say.

"No, your mother's right," says Dad. "You've obviously been getting in some extra practices, and it's paying off. Good job."

I shrug, although I have to admit it's nice to hear them say that. During our performance today, I actually *felt* the music as I was playing it, instead of just going through the motions.

Maybe it's possible for me to have my own thing going on and keep being a useful part of the Family McClintock. I still don't exactly love the music, but for some reason I've actually started to like playing it, more than I ever have before. It's a lot easier to be good at something that you enjoy.

It's also true that I've been practicing like crazy. Whenever I have a free second, I'm off in a corner somewhere with my guitar, working through my family pieces so they sound tight, messing around with the songs I'm playing with Sandy and Bert and even coming up with some new stuff of my own.

All the playing and practicing is starting to pay off. I really feel like I'm playing the best guitar of my life.

"Wow, Neil," says Bert one afternoon after I've pounded my way through our set. "You're going to show us up!"

"No way," I say. "We all sound awesome."

"Well, you sound extra awesome," he says. "Don't even try to deny it."

Sandy pushes some magazines and food wrappers out of the way and flops onto the couch. After the first couple of practice sessions, Bert gave up trying to keep the basement clean. Sandy doesn't seem to mind, and Beast is in his element.

"There's something missing," she says.

Bert and I turn to look at her.

"What do you mean?" I ask.

"I mean with 'Pass the Test,'" she says. "It's good, but it just sounds a bit...I don't know, not quite enough or something."

"I think I know what you mean," says Bert. "It needs some more *oomph*."

"*Oomph*?" I say. "What kind of *oomph*? The show is in six days. It's a little bit late to look for another musician."

"Not another musician," says Sandy. She jumps up from the couch and grabs her guitar. "Okay, listen, Neil. Remember when you asked me to try practicing with you guys? Well, I have an idea, and I want you to repay the favor and give it a shot, even if you really don't want to."

"Okay," I say, getting suspicious.

"I've been singing the lyrics to myself over and over," she says. "I think it would sound better if there were two singers on the chorus.

I'll keep singing lead the way I have been, but you come in on the chorus and do harmonies."

"But I can't sing," I protest.

"Don't give us that," says Bert. "We've both heard you."

Sandy starts strumming the chords on her guitar. "So when I sing this," she says, and she sings the first two lines of the chorus, "you sing it this way." She repeats the same two lines as harmony lines.

"I don't know," I say.

"Please, just try it," she says. "I helped you out, remember?"

"Fine," I say. "But if it sucks, I'm not doing it again."

"Fair enough," she says. "But you have to try for real."

I nod and reach for my guitar, but she holds out her hand to stop me. "Let's start simple," she says. "I'll run it through for us, nice and slow."

She starts playing, and once she gets past the intro, we both start singing. I'd expected it to be horrible, that I'd screw up the tune right away. Instead, I find that I'm able to sing a harmony line naturally, all the way through. The melody guides me, and I just do my best to sing along in a way that complements Sandy's voice.

We come to the end and Bert immediately starts clapping. "Awesome!" he says.

"Really?" I ask them.

"Sounded great," says Sandy.

"What did you think, Beast?" I ask, turning toward the couch, but he's in the process of killing a ninja and doesn't pay any attention to me.

"The real question is, what did you think?" says Sandy.

"It was okay," I say. She raises an eyebrow at me. "Okay, I admit it. It sounds better. We should do it with harmonies."

"Well, we better start practicing the new version," says Bert. "It's not like we've got much time left."

Ten

The *Welcome to Deep Cove* sign on the outskirts of town claims that we are home to eighteen hundred people, but Gran always says our true population is many times larger than that. During Deep Cove Days it definitely feels that way, as people who were born and raised here make the trek home from Ontario, Alberta and even farther afield. Many of them have been gone for a long time and have raised families and made lives for themselves elsewhere, but they still flock home in droves every year at the end of July to hang out with family and old friends.

Things always kick off with a parade on Monday morning. Shamus and Johnny will be marching with the Scottish Pipes and Drums band, so Mom and Dad cancel morning rehearsal, even though we're scheduled to play in the park in the evening.

I meet up with Sandy and Bert downtown, and we push through the crowds gathering on Main Street until we find a place to stand and watch the parade. It takes awhile because I keep running into people I know, and everyone wants to tell me how cool it is that we're going to be playing with Vince Beach.

"Jeez, Neil," says Bert. "You're an even bigger celebrity than usual."

"Whatever," I say, although I'm secretly pleased that Sandy is here to see me getting the attention. I know it's kind of conceited, but I can't help it.

People cheer as the parade approaches, led by the Pipes and Drums.

"I can't believe your brothers wear kilts for this!" says Bert as they walk past us.

"That's how it works," I say. I've made fun of them for that too in the past, but as they march by us, I feel a flush of pride. The music even sends a little chill up my spine when I remember that this is how my ancestors would have marched off to war.

As the first of the floats glides by, Bert shoves his way to the front of the crowd to compete with the little kids for the candy being thrown down to the street.

"You know," says Sandy, "I was so worried about coming here for the summer. I thought it would be super boring, hanging out with my grandmother and Bailey. I'm so happy that I met you guys."

"Yeah," I say. "It's cool." I really have to work on my vocabulary.

"I can't believe I'm going to sing in front of an audience," she goes on. "It's something I've always kind of wanted to do." She gives me a playful shove. "I guess I just needed to run into a professional musician to make it happen."

"Well, it was pretty much Bert's idea," I say. "I mean, the talent-show thing was his idea. You were my idea. I mean, your singing with us was my idea."

She laughs. "I know what you mean. Anyway, I'm really happy you asked."

I have trouble focusing on the rest of the parade. Floats and clowns and costumed kids on bicycles pass by us, but I keep looking out of the corner of my eye at Sandy. She stands next to me, clapping and cheering with the rest of the crowd, and I feel all light and goofy knowing that she actually wants to hang out with me.

When the last of the parade has gone by, the crowd dissipates and Bert comes back over to us, his hands full of candy.

"Check out this haul!" he says, shoving a Tootsie Roll into his mouth.

Sandy's phone buzzes, and she pulls it out of her pocket. "I gotta go," she says. "I have to meet Grandma and Beast for lunch. We're coming to your show tonight—see you there?"

"For sure," I tell her. "We should practice tomorrow too."

"Sounds awesome," she says. "I'm getting so excited! Can you believe it's happening in just three days?"

"I know," I say. "It's pretty crazy."

"Crazy awesome," says Bert. "We're gonna be rock stars!"

Sandy walks away down the sidewalk, turning to wave at us one last time.

"You gonna make a move on her or what?" Bert asks.

"I dunno," I say.

"Well, you're an idiot if you don't," he says. "I'm pretty sure she likes you."

"Really?"

"Well, she doesn't like me," he says. "And the only explanation for that is that she's already into someone else. Judging from the way she looks at you when we're playing, I'd say it's a safe bet."

I wonder what I'm supposed to do, or say, to find out if he's right. All I know is that it probably makes sense to wait and see what happens at the talent show.

"Man," says Bert. "I'd kill to be able to play guitar as good as you. Chicks love a guitar player. Stupid drums."

* * *

Since the first year we started performing, the Family McClintock has put on a show in the park during Deep Cove Days. We usually get a decent crowd, but this year the park is jam-packed.

"This is nuts," Shamus says to me as we're setting up the sound system on the makeshift plywood stage. "I can't believe how many people are here!"

"I know," I say. "You think they're really here just to see us?"

"Neil!" my father calls from behind the stage, where he and Mom are working out a set list.

I jump off the stage and walk over to them. "What's up?"

"Your mother and I have been talking," he says. "We both agree that you deserve some credit for all the extra practice you've been putting in."

"It hasn't gone unnoticed, Neil," Mom says. "You've been playing better than ever these past few weeks."

"Cool," I say. "Thanks."

"Question for you," says Dad. "Remember when you showed me that little riff you worked out for 'Off to the Dance'? You think you can still play it?"

"For sure," I say.

"Okay, good," he says. "I'll fill everyone in before we go onstage, but it should be pretty straightforward. We're just going to add four bars near the beginning, after Shamus comes in, and then you do your thing, and then Mom will come in the way she always does. Sound good?"

"Totally," I say. "Thanks."

Mom reaches out and pulls me in for a hug. "You're a big part of this team, Neil," she says. "You've definitely earned some spotlight of your own."

Before we go on, we huddle backstage and Dad quickly runs through the set list, taking a minute to explain the changes to "Off to the Dance." Then we climb onstage in the usual order. Mom and Dad go on first, followed by the twins, then Shamus and Kathy and finally me and Johnny. We all grab our instruments and take our places as the crowd gives us an enthusiastic welcome, full of hoots and hollers. Dad steps up to the mic.

"Welcome home!" he yells. Everyone cheers in response. "This is always our favorite concert of the year, and it's a great honor and a lot of fun to help kick off Deep Cove Days. So we hope you enjoy the show, and if you feel like dancing, you're in the right place!"

Things go off without a hitch. We start with "Off to the Dance," and when it's time for my new part, I step to the front of the stage and give it everything I've got, riffing and picking as quickly and energetically as I can. It's over in seconds, but when I'm finished and take a couple of steps back, the crowd cheers and claps for me. I'm used to hearing the crowd break out in applause when the twins dance, or Kathy sings, or Shamus, Johnny, Mom and Dad do their solos, but it's the first time I've heard applause directed straight at me. It feels awesome. I glance at Kathy, who winks at me and gives me a subtle thumbs-up.

The rest of the show is a doozy. I've got adrenaline coursing through my veins, and the rest of my family is obviously having as much fun as I am. When the girls are dancing, it's like they're floating on air. When Mom and Dad do a piano and fiddle duet, the music sounds pure and perfect. Even Johnny's pipes seem to have a mind of their own, blasting out confidently whenever they're needed.

Best of all is the audience. People are soaking us up, shouting and clapping and dancing in circles with each other. They scream so much at the end of the show that we give them three encores, the last songs of the night coinciding with a beautiful sunset. It's like something out of a movie. I glance down at one point and spot Sandy and her family near the front of the stage. She throws both her hands up and waves at me excitedly, as if she's been watching me this whole time, waiting for me to see her.

I'm on such a high after the show that I'm almost vibrating. I've been doing this for years, but for the first time I really feel like I'm a full member of the band. I don't even mind when Dad motions for us to follow him into the crowd when we're finished.

An old woman comes up to me and grabs me by both hands.

"I moved to Boston when I was sixteen years old," she tells me. "I used to come home every year, but after my husband died I stopped coming altogether. The last time I was home to Cape Breton was almost twenty years ago. I was worried that everything would be different. And it's so nice to learn that the important things have stayed the same."

She stops talking, and her eyes fill up with tears.

"You people keep the music alive," she says. "God bless you."

She glances past me and smiles, then leans in to whisper to me. "You know," she says, "girls love a good musician."

I turn around and see that Sandy is standing right behind me, waiting her turn.

"Thanks very much," I say to the lady. She smiles and pats me on the arm before moving away into the crowd.

I turn to Sandy. "What did you think of the show?" I ask.

She grins widely. "Are you kidding me?" she says. "You were so good, Neil. You were great the first time I saw you, but it was like you were possessed tonight!"

"Thanks," I say. "It was fun. Dad let me—" But I don't have the chance to finish, because she's leaning into me and kissing me, full on the lips, with all these people around. For a moment I don't know what to do, but I pull myself together and return the kiss.

She steps back and smiles. "I don't know why I did that," she says.

"It's okay," I manage to squeak out.

"Listen," she says. "I have to go. But we're going to practice tomorrow, right?"

"Definitely," I say.

"Okay," she says, and for a second we stand there smiling goofily at each other. "I'll text you tomorrow," she says. Then she disappears into the crowd.

I stumble back to the side of the stage, where a steady line has formed at Gran's merch table.

"I have to say, boy," says Gran as she counts out money and shoves T-shirts into bags, "I've seen every show you guys have ever done, and this was one of your best nights, hands down."

I have to agree with her. We've just finished one of our most awesome shows ever, I'm playing the best guitar of my life, in less than a week we're going to be opening for a music superstar, and the girl I like just made the first move on *me*. I doubt I've ever had a better night in my life.

Of course, it would be too much to ask for it to last.

Eleven

'm lost in my thoughts and don't realize that Dad is yelling for me until Gran pokes me in the arm and points him out. He's standing backstage with some man I've never seen before.

"Neil," says Dad as I walk up to them, "this is an old friend of mine, Martin Teasdale. He's the guy who helped us land the Vince Beach gig."

"Call me Marty," he says, shaking my hand.

"So you're their manager?" I ask him.

"No," he says. "I work for the promotions company that's coordinating the Halifax end of things. We were asked to find some local openers, and since I've been hearing good things about you guys, I decided to give your old man here a call. After what I just saw, I have to say I'm extremely happy I did. You guys were incredible!"

"Thanks," I say.

"Seriously," he goes on. "Just incredible. I can't wait to hear you on the big stage. I know Vince is going to love you guys. So how do you feel, Neil? Getting excited about Thursday? Nervous?"

For a moment I wonder how he's heard about the talent show. But that just doesn't make any sense.

"Thursday?" I repeat.

Marty laughs. "Of course you aren't nervous," he says. He turns to Dad. "I gotta say, you've raised a bunch of true professionals, McClintock. Listen, guys, I would love to hang out longer, but I have to drive all the way back to Halifax tonight, so I should hit the road. You know where you're going, right?"

"You bet," says Dad. "We'll be there bright and early."

"Good man," says Marty. He shakes Dad's hand and then reaches out and slaps me on the back. "See you guys on Thursday."

"Dad," I say as Marty walks away, my heart sinking into my stomach, "what does he mean, on *Thursday*?"

Dad gives me a funny look. "What are you talking about?"

"The Vince Beach show is on Saturday, isn't it? That's what you told us."

"Yeah, but I had the date wrong. I told you guys about the change the next day at rehearsal. It's been on the calendar for weeks, Neil."

My head starts to spin.

"But Thursday is supposed to be our day off," I say.

"Come on, Neil," says Dad. "You aren't going to turn this into a problem, are you? Not after the show we had tonight. You did a great job up there, buddy. I'm proud of you, but it was just a warm-up. Aren't you dying to get up in front of a really massive crowd on Thursday?"

I'm at a loss for words. I don't know what to do or how to explain to my father how horrible this is. Before I have the chance to say anything, he's hustled me around to the back of the stage and called the rest of the family over to help tear down our equipment. Next thing I know, we're packed up and driving home, and even though everyone else is chattering excitedly about the great show we've just had, I'm staring out the window of the bus, thinking about Bert and the Family McClintock and the Vince Beach Band and the awful way they've become tangled up with each other. Mostly, though, I'm thinking about Sandy and wondering if she'll ever talk to me again if I bail on the talent show.

"What's the matter with you?" Johnny asks me as we pull into the driveway. "You haven't said anything since we left the park."

"Nothing," I say.

"Yeah, right," he says. He leans in and whispers, "I saw you kissing that chick from the church show. Nice work. No wonder you're tongue-tied."

I look at him, and for a second I consider telling him what's happened, but then Dad parks and everyone piles out of the bus and starts to unload gear.

When everything's been put away, Dad locks the garage and we head into the kitchen to grab something to eat. Kathy and Gran drove home ahead of us, and they're pulling pizzas out of the oven and making a Caesar salad.

I'm starving and the pizza is delicious, and I'm happy to have something to focus on while around me my family laughs and talks. The more happy they sound, the less I can stand to listen to them, and I eventually manage to zone out completely. Then I hear my name being called from across the table, and I look up from my plate to see everyone staring at me.

"Earth to Neil!" says Kathy, laughing. "I just said your name about a dozen times!"

"Sorry," I say. "What is it?"

"I was just asking if you think we'll meet him."

"Who?" I ask.

"Vince Beach!" says Molly. "Do you think he'll let us hang out in his dressing room?"

"I don't know," I say. "I don't care about Vince Beach. He sucks."

"Jeez," says Shamus. "What crawled up your butt?"

I push back from the table and stand up, almost knocking my chair over in the process. Everyone looks startled. I'm so frustrated that I want to cry, but I don't know how to explain it to them.

"I hate country music!" I yell. "You all know I hate it, so why do you expect me to be excited about this stupid concert? I—I'm not coming to the show in Halifax. I can't do it!" I can't stand the way they're all looking at me, so I stare down at the table, clenching my jaw.

"Neil," says my mother, after a long moment. "What do you mean you can't do it? Of course you're coming with us."

"I'm not," I say, forcing myself to look at her. "I'm staying here and I'm playing in the talent show on Thursday."

"What?" says my father. "What talent show? What is going on?"

"It was supposed to be a surprise," I say. "Or a secret, I guess. Bert and I started a band with this girl that we know, Sandy. We've been practicing for weeks, and we're already signed up."

"Well, I'm sorry to hear that," says Dad. "But we're signed up for Vince Beach too."

"No," I say. "*You're* signed up for Vince Beach. I didn't sign up for anything. If you'd told me from the beginning that it was on Thursday, this never would have happened." I know that's not fair, that it's my own fault for not keeping up to date with the schedule, but I can't help saying it.

Mom and Dad exchange a long look across the table, and then Dad turns to me.

"I'm sorry, Neil," he says. "But it's not up for debate. We need you with us on Thursday."

"Why does everything come down to me?" I say. "What about everyone else? What about Kathy?"

"Neil!" she says.

"What are you talking about?" says Dad.

"Kathy might not even be here next year," I say. "Are you going to blame her for making us weaker? I doubt it!"

Everyone turns to look at Kathy, who stares at me with her mouth hanging open, shaking her head with disbelief.

"Kathy," says Mom, "what is he talking about?"

I don't stick around to listen. I turn and leave the house, grabbing the key to the garage on my way out. I let myself in through the side door, but I don't turn on any lights. I wait until my eyes adjust and then grab my guitar from the wall and drop into the beat-up old couch in the corner.

For a while I don't play anything. I just lie there in the dark with my guitar on top of me. I run my left hand up and down the frets, forming and reforming chords, while my right hand moves over the strings so lightly that no sound even comes out.

I'm not sure how long I lie there like that, but eventually there's a knock on the door and Gran comes into the garage. She switches a light on, and I put my arm up to block my eyes.

"You okay, Neil?" she asks.

"Not really," I say.

She comes over and pulls a stool up next to me.

"You know," she says, "I fell in love with your grandfather because he was such a wonderful musician. All the girls were after him back in those days." She looks at me and her eyes twinkle. "Girls love a man who can play music. It gets them all weak in the knees."

I allow myself to smile a little bit.

"Johnny told us about this girl you've been hanging out with," she says. "Is this the same girl you and Bert have been playing music with?"

"Yeah," I say.

"Well, she could sure do worse than the likes of you," Gran says. "Fine musician and a good-looking fella to boot."

"Yeah right," I say.

"What's that supposed to mean?" she asks. "You know you're the only one in the whole damn family who took after me."

I look at her and raise an eyebrow.

"Really," she says. "Take a close look at my wedding photo in the living room. Short and dark but awful cute, if I do say so myself. Your grandfather was a big tall redheaded hunk of a man, and his tough Scottish genes blasted right down into every one of my kids and then into every one of my grandkids." She reaches out and pokes me in the forehead. "Except for you."

I've never thought about that before, and I can't figure out why she's telling me now.

"Don't worry," she says, as if she's reading my mind. "I don't expect that hearing you look like your grandmother is going to do much to cheer you up. All I'm saying is that genetics is a funny business, and you never know who's gonna get what from whom. And this family is awful lucky, if you ask me, because every one of you got the gift of music, and that's something you'll be able to carry with you right through life."

"I guess," I say.

"It's true," she says. She gets up from her stool. "If you refuse to go to Halifax on Thursday, they'll get over it eventually. You don't need to worry about that. But I would expect the same is true of Bert and this Sandy girl. If they don't cut you some slack, they probably aren't very good friends to begin with."

That's not my biggest concern at the moment. "Did I get Kathy in trouble?" I ask.

"Nobody is in trouble," she says. "Kathy is in there talking things over with your parents. It's not a bad thing if this family starts to communicate a bit better." She walks back over to the door. "You could probably help out with that, so don't stay out here all night."

She leaves, and I force myself to sit up. I'm still holding on to my guitar, and I find myself strumming out the tune to "Pass the Test." I get through a couple of verses and then switch over to my piece from "Off to the Dance." I can't get into either song, so I stand up and hang my guitar back on the wall. Then I pull out my phone and stare at the screen for a minute before sending a message to Bert and then Sandy.

Bert texts me back almost immediately, with a string of swearwords and exclamation marks. Although I check my phone every five minutes for the next couple of hours, I don't hear back from Sandy at all.

Twelve

By Wednesday, I still haven't heard a word from Sandy, although Bert breaks down and calls me. He's still ticked off, but at least he's calmed down a bit. He tells me Sandy hasn't returned his messages either.

"I don't know why," he says. "It's not like I'm the one who screwed everything up."

"Thanks for making me feel better," I say.

"Sorry, buddy," he says. "You screwed up. What do you want me to say?"

At least Kathy doesn't hate me. I apologize to her so many times that she eventually has to tell me to stop.

"I wish you hadn't done it," she says, "but I'm happy that everything's out in the open now."

"So what's going to happen?" I ask.

She shrugs. "I don't know yet. I'll have to see how things play out when I get back to school. The important thing to remember is that the band will still go on, even if I'm not around next year. It'll just be a bit different. Mom and Dad realize that, and they aren't pressuring me either way, which is good."

I can't help wondering why they haven't taken it that easy on me, but that's just how it is, I guess. I can't be in two places at one time, so I do my best to forget about the talent show. It isn't easy, especially when I close my eyes and imagine kissing Sandy and realize that will probably never happen again.

Mom starts banging on our bedroom doors at five o'clock on Thursday morning. We line up outside the bathroom and wait our turn to take a five-minute shower, then wolf down breakfast and load the bus. By six thirty we're on the road for the four-hour drive to Halifax.

After we cross the causeway to the mainland, Dad pulls the bus over so we can grab some coffee and doughnuts. By this time we're starting to wake up, so when we get back on the road, he starts running through his plan for our set.

"Three songs doesn't give us a huge chance to make an impression," he says, "so we have to make the most of the time we have. We should definitely start with 'Off to the Dance.' It gives everyone a chance to do their thing, and it'll get the crowd riled up."

"Do you think Vince Beach is going to like us?" asks Maura.

"How could he not?" says Mom, turning in her seat and smiling back at us.

"Maybe he'll come out and do a song with us!" says Molly.

"I wouldn't count on that, girls," says Dad. "I'm sure he'll have a lot of preparing to do backstage. But you never know. Maybe he'll find a minute to hang out in the wings and watch us do our thing."

When we're an hour away from Halifax, Mom pops the latest Vince Beach CD, *American Saloon*, into the stereo and jacks the volume.

Even though I really don't like country music, it's hard not to get a little bit excited when everyone else in the bus starts singing along.

"*I bought a big old ring, and if you tell me yes, I'll rent a big ol' tux, you'll buy a big white dress.*"

By the time we spot the first sign for Halifax, I'm laughing and belting it out along with them.

"*We'll get a big old crowd, and have a big old night. We've got a future together, and it's big and bright.*"

The concert is on the Halifax Common, a large park in the middle of the city. Dad drives slowly past the fences that have been erected around the perimeter, looking for the talent and personnel entrance. It's slow going, and we're forced several times to stop in the middle of the road as steady streams of people move toward the concert grounds.

"This is nuts," says Johnny. "The show doesn't even start for three hours."

"I can't believe we're going to be playing for a crowd this big," says Kathy.

"They came to see Vince Beach," says Gran, "but they'll leave talking about the Family McClintock."

She sounds so sure of this that I start to think about what this concert could mean for us. We've been slowly building a name for ourselves over the years, but exposure like this doesn't come along very often. Although part of me still wishes more than anything that I could be in Deep Cove to play my debut show with Sandy and Bert, I'm happy for the first time in days, knowing that I'm going to experience this moment with my family.

Dad pulls up in front of a large gate and jumps out to talk to some security guards, then quickly gets back behind the wheel while they open the gates. As simple as that, we're in the backstage area. We park and get out of the bus. It's insane back here. The stage is huge, like nothing we've ever played before, and people with clipboards bustle about in all directions.

Molly squeals and points to a huge bus parked off by itself. The side of the bus is dominated by an image of an American flag blowing in the wind. Vince Beach's big grinning face is superimposed on top, sideburns, cowboy hat and all, and *American Saloon Tour* is written in a giant swoosh of glittery letters across the bottom. Two giant burly guys with goatees and sunglasses flank the doors to the bus.

"Wow," says Johnny. "His bus makes ours look like a tin can on wheels."

"I bet he's in there right now!" says Maura.

"Don't get too excited," says Shamus. "By the looks of those bodyguards, you won't get within spitting distance."

Dad calls out to a young woman who is hurrying past us, talking a mile a minute into a headset. She stops in her tracks and glances over at us impatiently.

"Hi there," he says. "I'm wondering if you know where I can find Martin Teasdale."

"He's with the local promoter?" she asks.

"That's right. We're one of the opening acts. The Family McClintock."

Her eyes do a quick scan of us, clustered together beside the bus. "I believe the local promoters have a table set up over there somewhere," she says. She points to the other side of the stage and then hurries away without asking if we need anything else.

"Let's you and me go find him," Mom says, putting her hand on Dad's back.

"You guys hold tight," says Dad to the rest of us. "We've got to grab the contract and find out from Marty what time we go on. We'll be right back."

"Come on, girls," Gran says to the twins. "No reason why we shouldn't get the two of you dressed for the show. It'll save us all a bit of time later on."

She and Kathy hustle them back onto the bus.

"You guys want to check out the sound setup?" asks Shamus. Johnny and I follow him through the chaos, making our way toward the stage. Next to a metal staircase that leads up to the back of the stage, three guys wearing Vince Beach T-shirts are standing around, laughing and smoking. They've got rolls of tape in different colors hanging from their belts, and one of the guys is talking into a walkie-talkie.

"I think those guys must be roadies," says Shamus. "They'll know what's going on."

He walks up to them, and they stop talking and turn to look at him.

"How's it going?" says Shamus.

"Can we help you?" one of the guys asks.

"We're one of the opening acts," says Shamus. "I was just wondering when we should start setting our gear up. Can we back our bus up here and unload?"

The guys stare at him for a second, then burst out laughing.

"Gear?" says one of the guys, a bald dude with a tattoo of a snake on the back of his head.

"Yeah," says Shamus, who is beginning to sound unsure of himself. "Our amps and cables and stuff."

The guys look at each other, amused. Two of them flick their cigarettes to the ground and walk away.

"Listen, man," says the tattooed guy. "You won't have to worry about your gear. Who did you say you guys were?"

"We're with the Family McClintock," says Shamus. "We're one of the opening acts."

"Yeah, well, you're not the only one, so get in line, Mr. McClintock," he says. "We've got more important things to deal with right now."

"You don't have to be such a jerk," says Johnny. Shamus turns and shoots him a look that says shut up, but the tattooed guy just laughs.

"You're right, dude. My apologies," he says. "It comes naturally. Listen, you don't have to worry about setup. You guys will plug into the sound system Vince is using. Just show up with your instruments when it's time to go on, and we'll take care of you."

"What about soundcheck?" asks Shamus.

"That should all be in your contract," says the guy. "I don't know anything about when you get a soundcheck. Don't worry about it though. We do this every day, and we're not gonna make the Family McClintock look bad."

"Okay," says Shamus. "Thanks."

"Man," says Johnny as we walk back to the bus. "What a bunch of meatheads."

"They're roadies," I say. "I think they're supposed to act that way."

"He's right," says Shamus. "I should've just let Dad figure that stuff out."

Molly and Maura are standing with Gran and Kathy beside the bus, practically vibrating with excitement. They're all dressed for the show, in matching tartan dresses, black tights and new dancing shoes.

"You guys look great," says Shamus, and they giggle excitedly.

"No sign of Mom and Dad?" I ask Gran.

"Not yet," she says. "They're dealing with the contract. I suppose that takes a while."

"They're probably getting a tech breakdown too," says Shamus.

"Hey, check it out!" says Johnny. "There's Vince Beach!"

He's pointing at the tour bus. Sure enough, the door is open and Vince Beach is standing on the bottom step, talking to his guards. The brown Stetson on his head casts a shadow over his aviator sunglasses. In his tight jeans and cowboy shirt, he looks every bit the country music star.

"You girls want to see if you can get his autograph?" I ask the twins.

"Yes!" they yell in unison, jumping up and down. Maura goes into the bus and comes back out with the *American Saloon* CD case.

"You sure that's a good idea?" asks Gran.

"What can it hurt?" I say. "How's he going to say no to those two? Besides, we're opening for the guy. That's gotta mean something."

"I'll come with you," says Johnny.

We walk over to the bus, and one of the guards turns around and puts his hand out to stop us. I look at Vince Beach, who is busy explaining something to the other guy and doesn't pay us any attention.

"What do you want?" asks the guard.

"Hi," I say. "We're one of the opening acts, and my sisters here were really hoping to get Mr. Beach's autograph."

Without even glancing at us, Vince Beach turns and walks back up the steps into the bus.

"Tell them to line up after the show like everyone else," he says over his shoulder before the door closes.

Molly looks like she's about to cry, and the guard softens a bit. "Don't worry, honey," he says. "Vince always needs time to concentrate before his shows. He'll be around backstage when the show is over, and you'll get to meet him then."

Johnny and I herd the twins back to the bus.

"What's the matter?" Kathy asks the girls when she sees their downcast faces.

"Vince Beach wasn't very nice to us," says Maura.

"What do you mean?" asks Shamus. "What did he say?"

"He didn't say anything," says Johnny. "He wouldn't even say hi to them."

"His bodyguard said he needs to concentrate," says Molly.

"What kind of grown man needs to concentrate so hard that he can't say hello to a couple of nine-year-old girls?" Gran says. "American buffoon, if you ask me!"

This gets a giggle out of the twins, and the mood lightens for a brief moment, until we see Mom and Dad striding toward us. They don't look happy.

"Unbelievable," says Dad, shaking a piece of paper.

"What's going on?" asks Shamus.

"You tell them," Dad says to Mom. "I'm too angry."

Martin Teasdale hurries up to the bus.

"Guys," he says, "I'm really sorry about all this. I don't know what to tell you."

"Why don't you start by explaining why we couldn't have learned about this a month ago?" says Dad. "Or three days ago, when you came to see us in Deep Cove."

Martin rubs his face. "I didn't know," he says. "You have to believe me. The Beach people kept telling us there were holdups with the contracts but that it would be no problem. I should have known better, but they were throwing around all kinds of legal talk, and they made everything sound legit."

Dad throws his hands in the air. "Marty, if I hadn't known you for twenty years, I never would have agreed to hold off on signing a contract," he says. "I should have trusted my gut."

"I know," says Martin. "I don't know what to tell you. I feel terrible."

"Will somebody please tell us what's going on?" says Gran.

"It turns out there isn't room for us onstage," says Mom. "Since we didn't pre-sign a contract, there's nothing we can do about it."

"What?!" I ask at the same time as everybody else.

"You mean we aren't on the program anymore?" asks Johnny.

"Not exactly," says Martin, who looks miserable. "We were informed this morning that opening acts couldn't exceed four individuals. That's not a problem with the other two acts we booked, but with you guys..." He trails off.

"Four!" says Kathy. "But there are eight of us!"

"Exactly," says Mom.

"But the stage is huge!" says Shamus.

"It's not the stage," says Marty. "It's the setup. There's no time to do a soundcheck, and we only have five minutes between acts. Now the tech guys are telling us they only have time to mic and line-in four people per show."

"Tell them the rest of it, Marty," says Dad.

"Apparently," says Martin, "Beach decided at the last minute that he wanted to bring his own opening act along with him. Some up-and-coming country starlet named Lula Burke."

"Omigod, we love her!" scream the twins.

"I bet Vince Beach loves her too," Johnny whispers to me.

"Anyway," Martin continues, "that means that for the local openers there will only be time for one song per act."

"So just to recap," says Dad. "No time for a soundcheck. No time for the three songs we've prepared. No room for the whole family."

"That's right," says Martin. "I am really, really sorry about this."

Dad looks at Mom. "Do we need to have a family huddle about this?"

She shakes her head. "I don't think so."

Dad holds the contract in front of him and rips it in half, then hands it to Martin.

"Sorry, Marty," he says. "The Family McClintock plays together or the Family McClintock doesn't play at all."

"I understand," says Martin. "I really wish it hadn't worked out this way."

"It's not your fault, my man," says Dad. "But if you happen to be speaking with him, you can let Vince Beach know that he can take his big old concert and his big old bus and shove them both up his big old—"

"Language!" says Gran.

Thirteen

"**N**eil," says Dad once we're back on the highway headed toward Deep Cove, "what time is the talent show?"

"What do you mean?" I ask.

"You heard me," he says. "I want to know if we can make it back to Deep Cove in time for your performance."

"It starts at two," I tell him. "There's no way we can get there in time."

"It's only noon," says Mom. "If we drive straight through without stopping, we can be home by four."

"There's no way it will be over by then," says Dad.

"It doesn't matter," I say. "I mean, I appreciate it and everything, but it won't work. Bert would probably do it, but Sandy hasn't spoken to me since I texted to tell her I had to cancel."

"Give me a break," says Johnny. "Are you going to give up that easy? That Sandy girl likes you. Why else would she have kissed you?"

"She kissed you?" asks Kathy.

"Ooooooh," say the twins.

"Guys!" I say. "Seriously, thank you, but I know the situation better than you all do. It's too late. It's not going to work."

"Neil," says Gran, "do you know what people said when your parents decided to form a family band? They said it wouldn't work. Now would you mind telling me where the Family McClintock is today?"

"Fleeing the Vince Beach show in a rusty government bus?" says Johnny.

"You're professionals," says Gran. "Every last one of you. Who cares what Vince Beach or the rest of those clowns back in Halifax think? All I know is that when you guys have the chance to play, you take it and you knock it out of the park. Just ask the crowd that showed up for your Deep Cove Days concert the other night. If you're serious about taking your talent in another direction,

Neil, you can't back down just because you hit a roadblock. You have to figure out how to get around it and keep going."

"She's right," says Shamus. "Call her."

The rest of them start chanting. "Call her! Call her! Call her!"

"Fine!" I exclaim. "Just stop yelling, please."

"You're going to call Sandy?" asks Kathy.

"I'll call Bert," I say. "I'll see what he thinks we should do."

Bert answers on the third ring. "Well if it isn't the guy who crushed my dreams," he says. "Are you calling from Vince Beach's backstage party room? Are the babes all over you?" he asks.

"Where are you?" I say.

"I'm in my basement," he says. "You want to know what I'm wearing?"

"Listen for a second," I tell him. "We aren't playing the Vince Beach concert anymore."

"What?" he yells. "Why not?"

"I don't have time to explain," I tell him. "But we're on our way back to Deep Cove right now. Have you pulled us out of the talent show yet?"

"No," he says. "I didn't bother, because they'll figure it out when we don't show up. Wait. Why?"

"Do you think we can convince Sandy to do it after all?"

"Are you serious?" he asks. "I don't know, man. She hasn't returned my messages. I guess it's worth a shot though."

"Try again," I tell him. "I don't think she'll answer my call."

"All right," he says. "I'll try, but I wouldn't count on it."

I hang up and wait to hear back from him. Nobody in the bus says anything as we fly down the highway.

When my phone dings with a text message, everyone turns to look at me.

"Who is it?" asks Shamus.

"It's Bert," I say. "We're on."

"Put the pedal to the metal!" yells Gran.

* * *

The stage for the talent show is set up in an empty lot close to the beach. The parking lot is full, and there are cars parked on both sides of the road. Dad slowly brings the bus to a stop at the edge of the crowd just as one of the acts finishes and walks offstage.

"Let's hear it for young ventriloquist Walter Willis and his hilariously nasty dummy, Willis Walters!" the announcer is saying as we get out of the bus. "Might be a good idea to take old Willis home and wash his mouth out with soap, Walter. Ladies and gentlemen, you'll notice if you turn around that Deep Cove's very own Family McClintock has just made a dramatic arrival to our show. Obviously they aren't eligible to perform today, but I understand that young Neil McClintock will be performing with a couple of his friends in just a little while. In the meantime, let's all put our hands together and give a big welcome to Claire Campbell, who will be using interpretive dance to tell the story of Deep Cove's founding, set to a medley of Motown classics."

Sandy and Bert push through the crowd to us, Beast in tow.

"You made it!" says Bert. "Atta boy, Neil. You didn't let us down after all!"

"Neil, I'm sorry," says Sandy, talking really fast. "I was really upset when you canceled, but I'm over it. You were just doing what you had to do."

"I'm glad you're not still mad at me," I say.

"Are you kidding?" she says. "I'm too excited to be mad."

"Are you guys ready for the big debut?" asks my mother.

"I think so," says Sandy. "I'm a little nervous though."

"Me too," I say.

"What are you talking about?" asks Bert. "You've been doing this since you could barely walk."

"No," I say, turning to point at the bus. "I've been doing *this* since I was born. Getting onstage with you guys is totally new territory."

"We should get over there," says Sandy. "We're on in a couple of acts."

I grab my guitar from the back of the bus, then stop in front of my family.

"I'm happy you guys are here," I say.

"The only way we'd miss this is for a previously scheduled engagement," says Dad.

Kathy leans in to hug me, Johnny gives me a thumbs-up, and as I start to walk away they all yell after me together.

"Good luck!" I hear them say, in one big voice.

We walk through the crowd and stand by the back of the stage, where Bert has stashed his drums.

The dancer finishes her performance and takes a bow, then skips off the stage to a smattering of applause as the announcer walks back to the mic.

"Let's hear it for Claire," he says. "Next up, the a capella stylings of the Deep Cove Boyz, or DCB. Come on up, fellas."

Three high-school seniors in tracksuits climb the steps and break into a harmonized rendition of "Bohemian Rhapsody," complete with beatboxing. The announcer signals to us from the corner of the stage. "You're next," he mouths.

"Oh my god," says Bert. "I can't believe this is happening."

"Neither can I," says Sandy. "But I'm glad that it is."

"I need to ask you a question," says Bert. "Why didn't you respond to me when I was trying to get in touch with you? It wasn't my fault—Neil was the one who canceled."

"I know," she says. "I'm sorry. If you want to know the truth, I have a crush on Neil, and I was really upset that he chose the other gig. Then I was kind of embarrassed and I just didn't want to talk about it."

Beast pretends to barf, and as I feel the heat rise up through my face, I wonder if my genetic resistance to blushing is failing me after all this time.

"Fair enough," says Bert, turning to wink at me.

"Wait!" says Sandy. "What are we going to call ourselves?"

"Oh no!" says Bert. "I forgot all about that."

"I might have an idea," I say. I tell them what I've been thinking.

"It's perfect!" says Bert.

"Totally," says Sandy. She leans down and whispers something to Beast, who nods.

The Deep Cove Boyz finish their song with a huddle and then run offstage, pumping their fists. The announcer gestures for us, and we climb onto the stage, carrying pieces of Bert's drums. I'm helping him set up when he glances into the crowd and his face goes white.

"What's the matter?" I ask him.

"Mrs. Klein is here," he says. "What are we going to do?"

"What are you talking about?" I say. "We're going to do the song, and nobody will ever know what it's about."

"I don't know, man," he says. "Part of me wants to scream to the world that I wrote it for her."

"Try to restrain yourself," I tell him.

I plug in my guitar, the announcer hands Sandy a mic, and suddenly we're standing in front of an audience and ready to roll. I've been onstage more times than I can count, but I've never been this nervous.

"All right, ladies and gents," says the announcer. "I believe we're all set up and ready for our final act. So let's give a big Deep Cove—hang on a second." He hurries over to us. "What do you guys call yourselves, anyway?" he whispers.

Sandy points at Beast, who is standing at the bottom of the steps, staring up at us. "Can you get my brother to introduce us?"

The announcer beckons for Beast to come onstage, then crouches next to him.

"Turns out that this young man is going to do the honors," he says to the crowd. "What's your name, buddy?"

"Beast!" he yells, and the audience cracks up.

"You ready to introduce your sister's band?"

Beast nods, and the announcer hands him the mic. "Whenever you're ready, Beast."

Beast looks out at the audience and then back at us, and for a second I worry he's going to freeze. Then he opens his mouth and, with the rage, tone and energy of a seasoned metalhead, screams out at the top of his lungs, "PUT YOUR HANDS TOGETHER FOR UNRELATED!"

"One-two-three-four," says Sandy into the mic, and then Bert smashes us into the song and we're doing it, we're finally playing something that I helped write.

The audience seems to be digging us. I have no idea if we'll win the talent show or not, but in this moment I don't care one bit. When we get to the first chorus and I lean in to harmonize with Sandy, I hear an extra-loud cheer from the back of the crowd, and I see my entire family standing by the bus, Molly on Dad's shoulders, Maura on Shamus's. They're screaming and clapping for me, and right now I know for sure that as great as it is to have a big family to make music with, it's even better to know that they're always ready to back you up when you most need it.

Acknowledgments

A huge thank-you to my wonderful family and amazing friends for their support, encouragement and enthusiasm. Thanks so much to everyone at Orca for being such a pleasure to work with, and in particular to my editor, Sarah Harvey, for her faith in my abilities and her significant insight into the craft of writing. A big shout-out to the hardworking musicians and performers of Cape Breton for sharing their gifts with the world. Finally, thank you a million times over to Andrew, who made all of this possible.

TOM RYAN was born and raised in Inverness, on Cape Breton Island. Like most transplanted Cape Bretoners, he spends a lot of time wishing he was back on the right side of the causeway. He currently lives in Ottawa, Ontario, with his partner and dog. He can be found online at www.tomwrotethat.com.